# CALM DOWN & Carry the F★CK ON!

## SWEAR WORD COLORING BOOK FOR ADULTS

TWYSTED COLORING BOOKS

Be Strong
& Kick Ass!

BASTARD

PEOPLE
LIKE YOU
ARE THE REASON
WE HAVE A
MIDDLE
FINGER

SMILE,
ASSHOLE

DICKHEAD

Today is
going to be
FUCKING
AWESOME!

YOU! YES YOU!
FUCK YOU.

I'M FRESH
OUT OF
Fucks
TO GIVE

DUMBASS

GO
WITH
THE
FUCKING
FLOW

KISS MY ASS

Shit
COULD BE
WORSE!

WANKER

FANCY
AS FUCK

BLOW
ME

FUCKNUGGET

IT'S FUCKING
COMPLICATED

DIPSHIT

No really...
IT'S ADORABLE
WHEN YOU THINK
I GIVE A SHIT

BITCH
DON'T TEST ME

eat
SHIT!

IT IS WHAT IT IS,
Fuck what it was.

SLUT

SCUMBAG

JIZZMONGER

CHILL THE
FUCK
out!

Cheers
BITCHES

TOTAL
PRICK

CUNT

MORON

Shithead

FUCK BOY

FAN
Fucking
TASTIC

BUTTHOLE

COCK
BURGER

CUM
GUZZLING
GUTTER
SLUT

TRAmp

ASSWIPE

MY PARENTS
SAID I COULD BE
ANYTHING.
So I
BECAME AN
ASSHOLE.

FUCK
YOU
VERY
much